Deer, Tree, the Shaman, and the Sun

A Story About Learning To Be Ourselves in a New World

JAMES K. PAPP

DEER, TREE, THE SHAMAN, AND THE SUN:
A Story About Learning To Be Ourselves in a New World

JAMES K. PAPP

Front cover photograph "Deer and Tree on Sun Mountain" by James K. Papp
All other art, photographs, and text by James K. Papp
(except for the quotation on page 13)

Book design: Bob Paltrow Design with Becky's Graphic Design®, LLC

Publisher: Planet Papp, LLC - James K. Papp and Lisa E. Papp
PO Box 29017, Bellingham, Washington 98228-1017 USA

Printed in the United States of America

ISBN: 978-0-9832041-7-6 (Paperback)
ISBN: 978-0-9832041-6-9 (Hard Cover)
ISBN: 978-0-9832041-5-2 (ebook)

Library of Congress Control Number: 2021911926

www.inquirewithin.com
mail@inquirewithin.com

To the storyteller in each of us:
May you be blessed with beauty,
with grace, and with love.

THIS MANDALA OF FLOWER PETALS WAS ARRANGED BY THE AUTHOR AS A PRAYER AND AN OFFERING OF THANKS TO SPIRIT, AND TO THE ANCIENT FOREST HE COMMUNES WITH NEAR HIS HOME.

Acknowledgments

I give heartfelt thanks to the following individuals
for their presence during the creation of this story,
during a truly memorable passage in time:

Joni Papp. . . . . for sharing expansive wilderness pilgrimages.

Diana Falconi. . . . . for illuminating timeless teachings.

Malcom Carter. . . . for inspiring soulful storytelling.

Roby James . . . . . . for graceful editing and understanding.

Nikki Jefford. . . . . . for energizing administrative support.

Lisa Papp. . . . . for loving and joyful companionship.

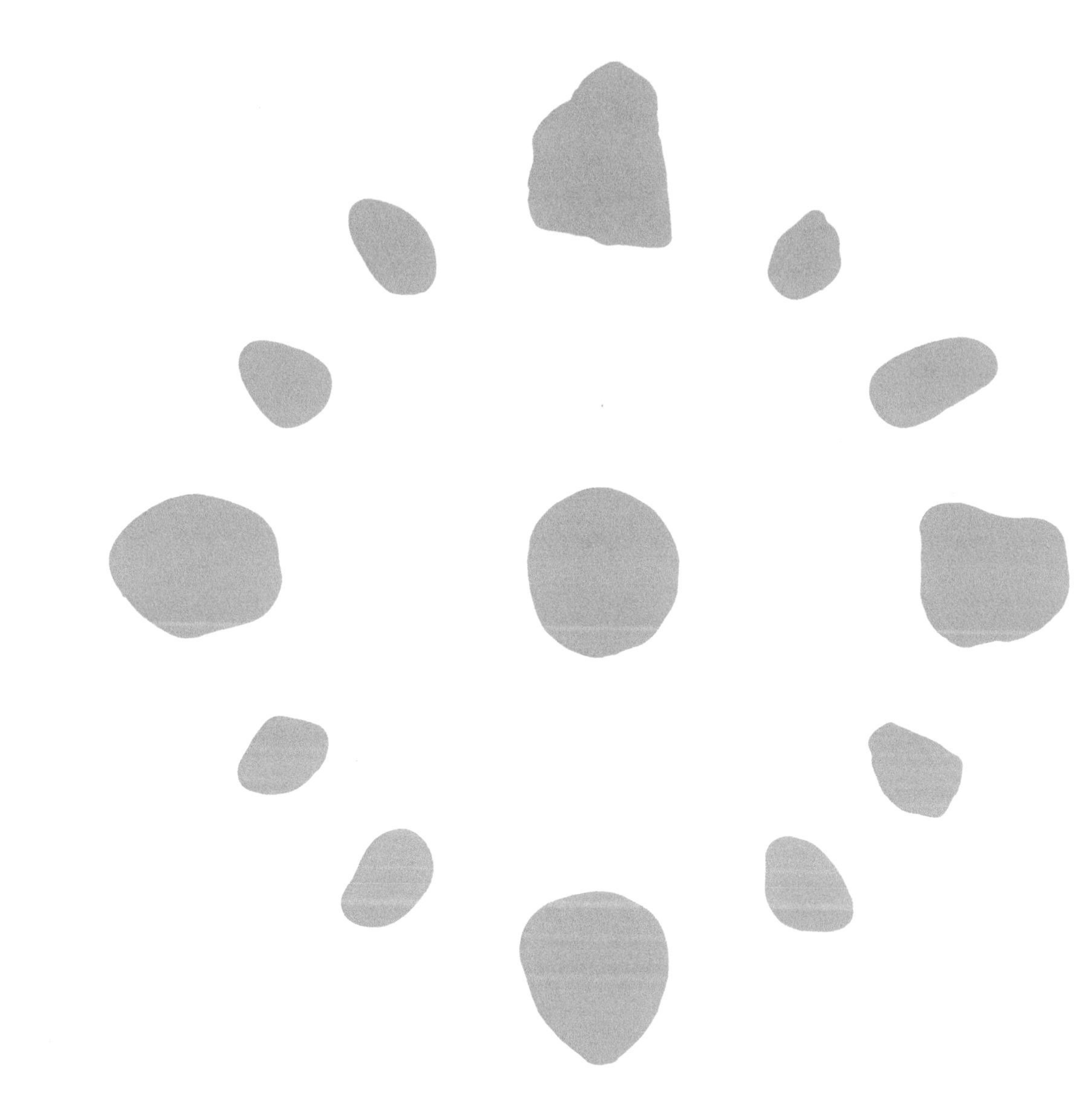

PART ONE

Once upon a time there was a shaman who was raised by Nature, in the Far North on Planet Earth. Ever since he could remember, the shaman's center—his peace and his power—was restored by being with the trees and the mountains, with the birds and the sky. Nature was always there and unfailingly supported his healing and harmony.

One year, some very strange events occurred that were life-changing for the people on Earth. At the center of these strange events was an illness that, whether you contracted it or not, and whether you believed it was real or not, rippled throughout human culture, profoundly disrupting it. Whatever you thought or believed or felt, you were touched by this disruptive phenomenon in some way.

The shaman watched a tidal wave of worry and fear propagate through communities all around the globe. So many activities and enterprises closed that a circuit breaker of humanity had been thrown—the momentum of constant progress halted. It was as if whatever "normal" used to be no longer existed. Constraints appeared at every turn— on eating, shopping, recreating, traveling, and working, even getting married and being buried. Warnings and restrictions were posted everywhere in many mediums, and a mutation of mask-wearing abounded. Many citizens of Planet Earth were consumed in the fires of this unexpected epidemic, which was much more than a physical sickness as it infected all aspects of society. Perhaps it was an illness born of being out of balance with Nature.

Saturn, Jupiter, and the Milky Way from Sunny Camp, Pasayten Wilderness, Washington

Sunny Pass, Horseshoe Basin, Pasayten Wilderness, Washington

The shaman knew that Mother Earth and Father Sun were the true parents of all the children on Earth – all of the animals, all of the plants, and all of the human beings. It occurred to him that human beings had not lived enough in harmony with each other and with Earth and had forgotten they were part of Nature. "There are so many of us, and we are placing such a collective load on Earth," reflected the shaman, "it is as if we have caused a rash upon our dear planet and we don't even know it. Yet saying that in front of all who are suffering would be insensitive and uncompassionate. Oh, what to do?"

The shaman realized that for him the answer was simple, as it always was - go and be with Nature, and then go from there. He would frolic with the trees and be with the mountains and the meadows. He would restore his balance and harmony in this way and see where it led. The shaman remembered what his sister had once told him on a wilderness pilgrimage: "We're not getting away from it all, we're getting back to it."

The shaman left the city and retreated to a distant wilderness parkland at the far edge of his home region. To trek into such a remote place made the shaman feel joyful and grateful. In this world outside the gravitational pull of civilization, he sighed...for days. It was a revelation to move beyond the bounds of a consensual reality that was gripping so tightly such a powerful archetype of death, of loss, and of utter aloneness.

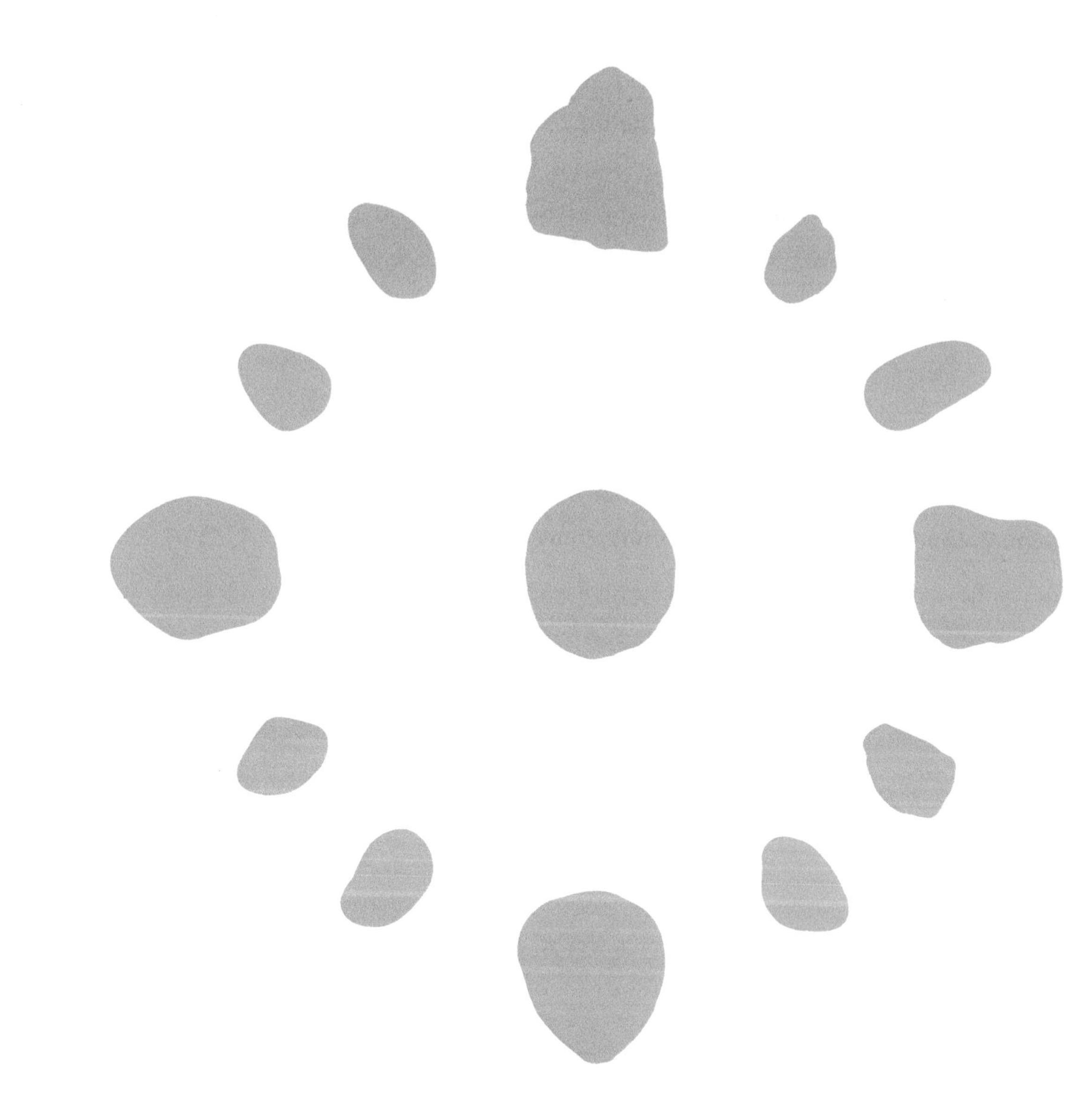

PART TWO

The Border Peaks from Yellow Aster Butte, Mount Baker Wilderness, Washington

Auspicious signs appeared at the shaman's stealth camp, tucked into the trees above a small lake in a meadow between rolling mountains. Hummingbird hovered repeatedly and fluttered excitedly, welcoming him. Deer encircled his camp, creating a magical zone of protection. Tree regaled him, sheltering and shading him and giving him company. Flower, in bright robes of red and yellow and blue and purple, serenaded him with melodies of pure joy. Wind strongly announced itself as an ally to cleanse his mind.

The shaman recalled what a wise sage wrote a very long time ago about how the universe is everlasting:

> *The reason the universe is everlasting is that it does not live for Self.*
> ~ **THE WISDOM OF LAOTSE, TRANSLATED AND EDITED BY LIN YUTANG**[1]

"The world of human beings is not going to return to what it was before this great disruption," realized the shaman. "And why should it, if the old world was not serving all species in all kingdoms on this planet? Why should the old ways of being that hurt so many of our fellow sisters and brothers continue exactly as they were?"

---

1   *Edited by Lin Yutang, The Wisdom of Laotse (New York, Random House, 1948).*

The shaman ascended a mountain above the lake. He was going to make an offering, a prayer that he might do his part as a planetary citizen to participate in the birthing of the new world that was already coming to be. At the wide-open summit, inside a cairn built with large rocks on the highest promontory, he deposited a quartz crystal as he prayed. It was a beautiful, brilliant stone that nearly filled the palm of his hand. Its multiple points spoke to him of interdependence, relationship, and community.

"Oh Great Spirit," he intoned softly, "thank you for guiding me to this sacred place. Dear Mother Earth, thank you for supporting me. Please receive back this crystal as an offering from my heart, as a prayer for harmony, for respect, for joy, and for peace, for all of us. May I artfully embody and express these qualities as we human beings participate together in the birth of a new world, a new era. May the Blessings BE!"

In placing the crystal deep in the cairn, built by human hands long ago, the shaman was adding a new piece to the story. Along with the quartz he set a small piece of wood from another continent far to the south, to honor his teachers who came from the south. "Thank you, dear teachers, for showing me how to walk with more lightness on this good Earth. Thank you for inspiring me to share more lightness with others. Thank you, thank you, thank you." Surveying the austere, sweeping summit of what he called Flower Mountain, the shaman cried out, "What a blessed day when the single best thing I can do is what I am doing today!"

Ascending Armstrong Mountain, Pasayten Wilderness, Washington

Comet Neowise under the Big Dipper, Pasayten Wilderness, Washington

The shaman ever-so-slowly made his way back down Flower Mountain, lingering at every turn. Blossoms in every direction danced in the talkative wind. Lichen-encrusted rocks peered out of the vast grassy meadows that curved out of sight toward his camp. Fluffy, cotton-ball clouds drifted across the deep blue sky, sending shadows up and down the mountains that ringed the large basin below. Butterflies flitted, and the little lake glittered like a pool of jewels in the late afternoon sun. In this sublime place, the shaman came to know himself in a new way.

The shaman slept that night under a blanket of pulsing stars and gleaming planets with "the comet that heralds" blazing under the great dipper near the northern horizon. While the night approached freezing in his tiny tent, he dreamed. In the dream, every single human being had a story to tell. Each individual could tell whatever story they wanted, and they could change the story whenever they wanted. Each individual allowed everyone else's story to be told completely, in its full integrity. Every human being on Earth expressed themselves without interruption or contradiction and felt respected and honored. A diamond-like clarity appeared in the eyes of each storyteller at the conclusion of their story, and the sparkling eye-glow spread one story at a time around the world.

The shaman woke up with a start. "Oh my god," he said, "we are all shamans."

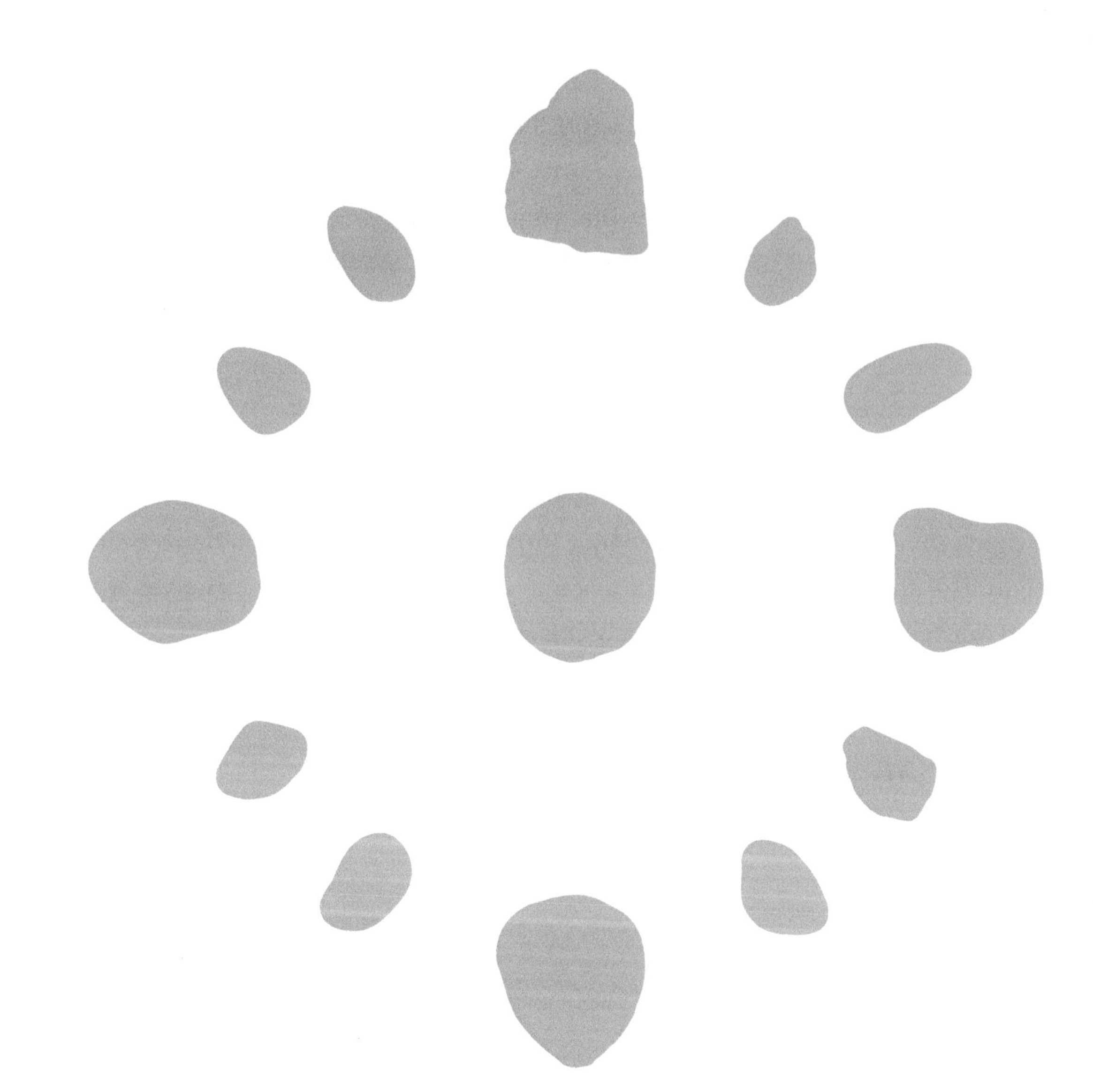

PART THREE

In the morning, the shaman went for a long walk on a gently winding forest trail that led past ponds and streams and through flower fields beyond counting. Last night's dream kept bubbling up through the day. All those stories told around the world would release and begin to process a vast reservoir of emotions and experiences.

Bits and pieces of our story are told each day, saw the shaman, particularly in how we react to our experiences in life. "How I choose to respond and to define myself are intertwined with the act of telling my story." A train of insight followed. "Learning ways to change our reactions to life experiences and to manage our energy profoundly supports us so we can rewrite our story to one that resonates in our heart of hearts. Conversely, the act of telling a new story directly influences how we respond to our experience of being alive. And within our heart is the compass we need that will guide us along our own unique path of healing within the current worldwide upheaval."

The shaman's head was spinning. "Listening to, or better yet—allowing—the stories of others to be told places us in respectful relationship with one another. In this resonant space, all of our ideas and opinions can be shared, and those which support what is truly "essential" for all creatures in all kingdoms—with grace—can now lead us as we work to right our relationship with Nature—as we work to right our relation with our self as part of Nature."

Indian Paintbrush, Pasayten Wilderness, Washington

That night Deer came to the shaman in his dream. He was hiking up a steep mountain trail in the forest with a heavy pack and met Deer coming down the trail. The shaman pulled aside that Deer might pass. Deer approached quietly, without fear, stopped to look directly into the shaman with gentle eyes of kindness, and said, telepathically, "I love you." Then her eyes transformed into the same unmistakable sparkling diamond eye glow that the storytellers had acquired. Deer disappeared down the trail toward the valley, and suddenly the shaman's backpack seemed to weigh nothing.

In his dream, the shaman glided upward on the trail to crest a ridge and, through a window in a stand of evergreens, he saw the sun rise, sending golden beams of light to illuminate the trees, the rocks, the ferns, the moss, and him – everything was glowing with some kind of inner light. It was as if everything were made of tiny, granular pieces of sun. Some sort of circuit connected every individual thing with the sun, circulating light between them. The shaman stared at the scene, entranced, and the sun transfigured into a candle and he seemed to be sitting on the cushion in front of his altar at home, staring into what he "knew" was a representative of the sun.

Deer and Tree on Sun Mountain, Washington

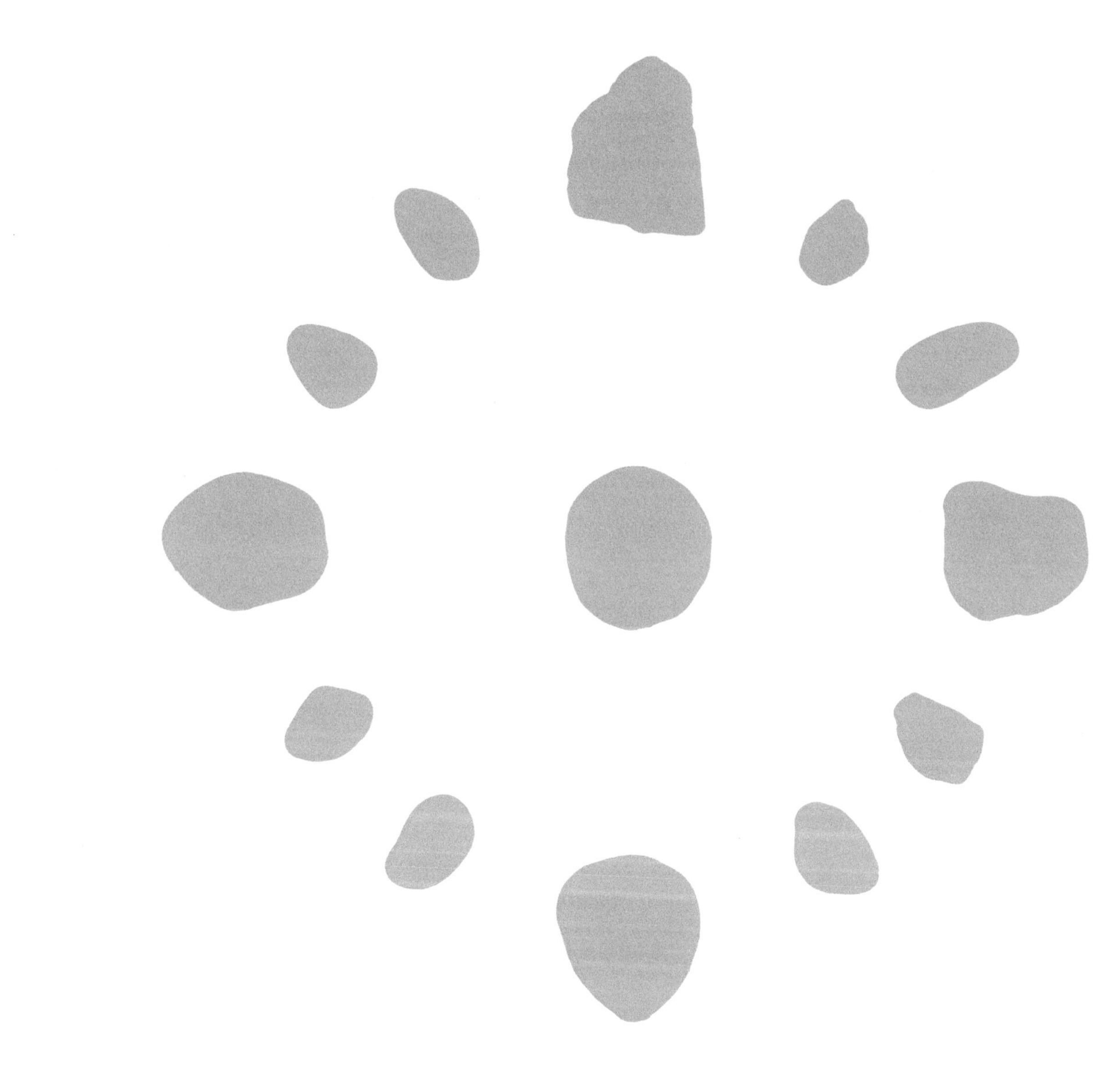

PART FOUR

Morning Sun on the North Butte, Chuckanut Mountain, Washington

The day drew near for the shaman to return home. To be reunited with his dearest companion would be a joy for both of them. With his wilderness renewal feeling complete, he cast his mind to those back home – friends, family, colleagues, acquaintances – and then he cast wider, to public figures and to those he had never known or even heard of, all around the world. He felt how much he loved them – all of them – regardless of what their story was. "We are all pieces of the sun," he mumbled to himself, "all our bodies come from the same Earth."

The shaman contemplated the goodness that had emerged from the worldwide disruption. Despite the suffering and loss, worry and upending, he saw so much compassion, so much love, and so much nobility as people helped one another. And during this stalling of constant human activity around the globe, the load lessened a little upon our dear mother, the Earth. People experienced clearer air and quieter skies and were able to reflect on their lives.

"What a blessing for each of us to have an opportunity to discover, in our heart of hearts, what is truly essential for us, whether that activity is available to us now or if it blossoms later," thought the shaman. "What does the compass in our heart of hearts point to, now that we must live in a new way? How can we all learn to be ourselves in a new world?"

I t occurred to the shaman that humanity was undergoing a huge initiation, a planetary rite of passage, as if we were on an unexpected and unknown road together. He remembered a friend's metaphor; we have disassembled, and now we are reassembling, but we won't reassemble in exactly the same way as we were before. "A new, more holistic perspective on life is emerging about being together on the planet," reflected the shaman. He retired to his tent for the night. Tomorrow he would make the trek toward home.

That last night, the shaman dreamed again under a glittering blanket of blinking stars. In his dream he gazed up at the Milky Way straight through his tent. Then there was no tent, and he was lying in a meadow surrounded by multi-hued, heavenly scented wildflowers. Stars appeared beside and then below him as well. He was rising and floating on a tiny meadow island with flowers and grasses and mosses as his stellar companions.

There was something more mysterious than usual about the Milky Way. The river of stars undulated and stretched and grew tributaries. It shapeshifted into a gigantic tree in space and from his meadow oasis he could see the whole tree, its branches, trunk, roots, and all. A wave of light rippled through everything and the shaman was lying under a mini-version of the tree, though it was still massively large compared to him. He recognized it as from a grove of evergreens he frequented near his home.

Midnight at Loudon Lake, Horseshoe Basin, Pasayten Wilderness, Washington

An Ancient One, Mount Baker-Snoqualmie National Forest, Washington

The cosmic tree, now cloaked in the appearance of an ordinary evergreen, pulsed with low bubbling tones. The tones had a rhythm, and the rhythm formed a cadence that sounded strangely familiar as it got louder. Then the shaman heard it: a message.

"We need you and you need us. Only you can stop the destruction that leads to the end of our mutual existence. We, the trees, your sisters and your brothers, are here to help you to re-establish balance and harmony with Nature, for the benefit of all of us. We cleanse the air and do so much more, yet you continue removing us from the face of the Earth. Your wellbeing depends on our continued existence, and our wellbeing now depends on yours.

"Come be with us in this time of need. Place your hands and your heads upon us that our far-reaching roots may deliver your worries and fears deep into the Earth, that we may help you stabilize and root yourselves during this time of great change. Our great-grandmothers and grandfathers, born before your renaissance, know how to endure. Come and share in our long world that all may thrive, that all may be here to participate in the birth of the new era, the era that benefits all creatures in all kingdoms for all time."

The shaman awoke with a stream of words echoing in his head: "There is no illness—there is only imbalance. Let us be with Nature. Let us go within to rediscover our own Nature. Let us explore the vast mystery of our own existence and experience the gloriously exquisite and graceful beauty and bounty of our own being. Let us remember who we are, and we will be gratefully together in unity; we will know together what to do. The healing, the wholeness, the harmony, are all thankfully, blessedly within us."

The shaman imagined all the storytellers as walking trees, with windows-of-the-soul eyes glowing with diamond-like clarity, radiating love. He imagined each of them growing their love and holding gently, like a newborn baby, the entire world in their heart.

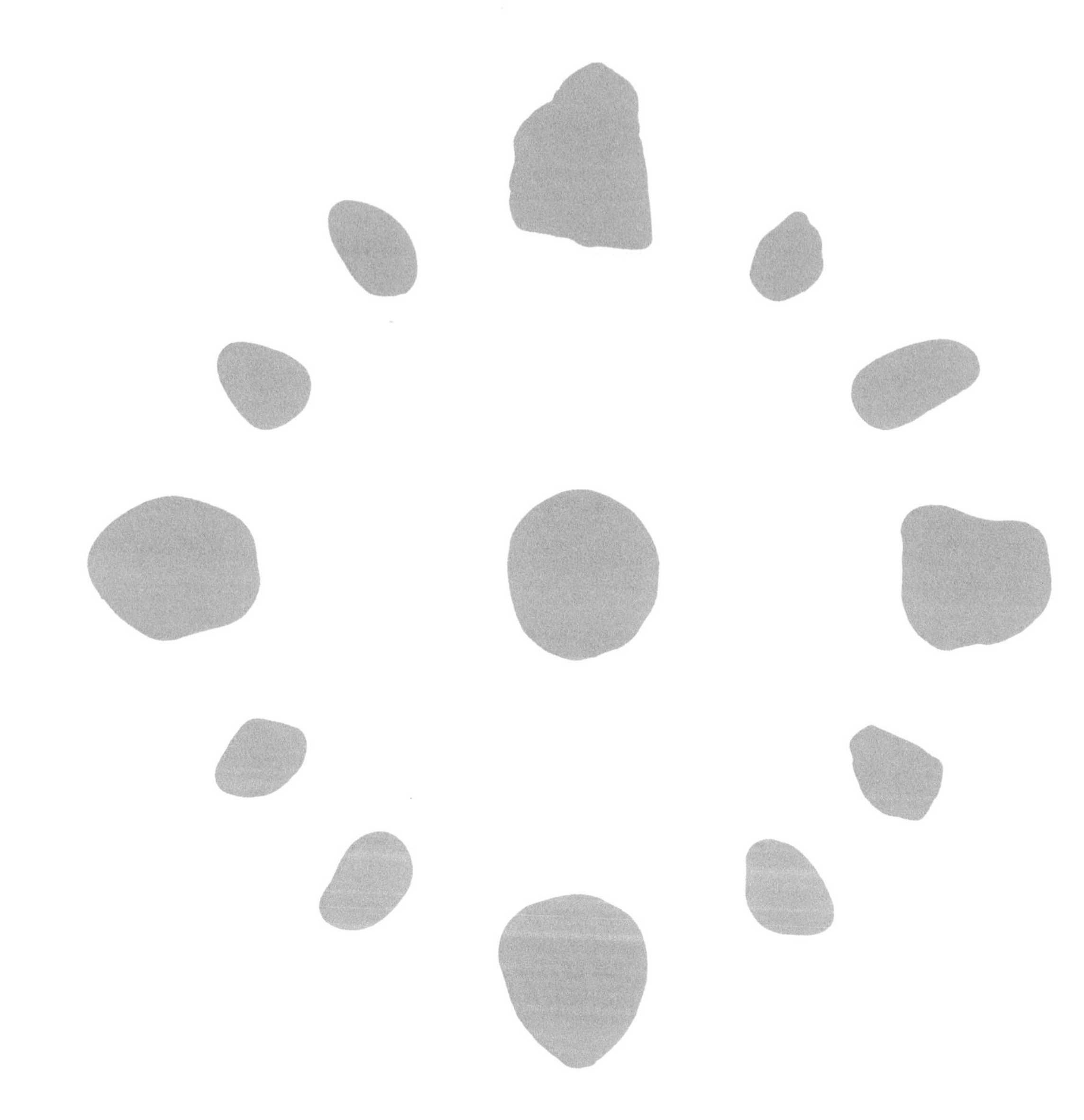

PART FIVE

When he arrived home from his wilderness communion, an idea popped into the shaman's head. He gathered a small group from his community, and they traveled together to be with the old trees that lived in a valley within the reaches of the local mountain range. As the pilgrims stood at the trailhead that led into the forest, they faced the wild trees, and the shaman made a small prayer, expressing gratitude for being there and asking the spirit of the place for permission to enter. After a short walk past lush ferns and large trunks, they reached their destination.

It took all ten of them to encircle the ancient grandmother tree, a survivor of fire and storm and industry. The cosmic tree, cloaked in an ordinary appearance, had a huge human-heart-shaped burl with roots cradling it and resembling veins and arteries. Having ringed the tree by holding hands, the ten pilgrims made a prayer of thanks to the tree and to all trees, and to Earth, for supporting them and for supporting all in the Web of Life. "Thank you, dear Mother Earth, for giving us our bodies, for feeding us, for clothing us, and for sheltering us. Thank you, in the end, for receiving our bodies back into yours that they may provide sustenance to others in the great and mysterious circle of life and death. Thank you for this communion. Thank you, thank you, thank you."

Afterward all were quiet and inward. A slight breeze caressed their foreheads, and sunlight cast small rays that filtered down through the canopy to dapple the forest floor. Later the ten would discover that at that moment, each of them felt something magical might happen.

Grandmother Tree, Mount Baker-Snoqualmie National Forest, Washington

Mount Baker-Snoqualmie National Forest, Washington

"We are storytellers," began the shaman. "The story we tell influences our experience of being alive, and how we react to our experience influences our story. What do you dare to dream of? What do you dare to lovingly let go of? How do you want to experience life in your heart of hearts? Now that we have come into harmonious communion in this blessed place, it is time for each of us to share our story."

It was like his dream. Each storyteller told their story, uninterrupted and with complete attention from their listeners, their witnesses. Emotions poured out in powerful rivers of feeling. Hopes were planted and fears were released. Shyness and unevenness gave way to noble integrity as each storyteller revealed more and more of who they were. A lucid, sparkling clarity appeared in their more-present-than-ever eyes. Then they were silent once again.

"The ancients tell us that we are walking trees," commented the shaman. "Maybe we are talking trees, too." He laughed. "Now here is a story that comes from the trees themselves… It goes…like this…"

The Trees that Talked

We speak to you now as ones who, like you,

are much younger than the mountains.

Sustained by the same water and the same sun

and both blessed to be in this place of wonder,

we have been asked to tell you to share and celebrate

this garden with your kind.

The bear brings you power, the deer protection.

We the trees, standing silently in witness, give you trust.

The water comes and goes.

The animals are busy on their own paths.

The mountains, well, they have other things to do,

communing with the very forces that created the face of this earth.

We speak to you now as ones whose lives come and go,

much like yours.

You, however, are affecting how this garden grows,

and that is why we seek your attention.

In Memoriam, Mount Baker-Snoqualmie National Forest, Washington

Grandfather Tree, Fisher Lake, Alpine Lakes Wilderness, Washington

Some years later, it was as if a seed had been planted in those ten people, and they had carried that seed everywhere they traveled. Gatherings around trees to give thanks and tell stories had spread throughout human culture all around the world, kind of like a virus. Important human events like marriages and memorials often occurred within the sacred space created by the trees. Human beings remembered more and more that they were the children of Father Sun and Mother Earth, and that all creatures in all kingdoms were their siblings. They remembered and rekindled the value of being grateful, especially for the lives of plants and animals taken for their sustenance. They began to learn, as their ancestors wisely knew so long ago, to take only what they needed and to leave the rest. It became common knowledge that the balance resulting from being in harmony with Nature—as part of Nature—is a vital source of wellbeing that supports a wondrously satisfying walk of years upon Planet Earth.

The shaman reflected on all that had occurred. So much had changed since his childhood in the Far North. A tidal wave of worry and fear had transformed into emanations of understanding and peace. He felt even more love in his heart than before. The changed world that was like a newborn baby cradled in the hearts of all had grown into a toddler and was learning to once more walk along the ancient paths.

May the Blessings BE!

JAMES K. PAPP'S art is inspired by mystery and awe. The camera and pen are magical portals for him to connect more deeply with the world. His work honors connection with Nature as our ally to cultivate more harmony in life.

Born and raised in Fairbanks, Alaska, James first kept a journal when he was a child. At right is an entry made when he was age six. His four decades studying metaphysics and spirituality include learning from Mayan spiritual teachers and a shaman in the Q'ero Andean tradition.

James is a loving husband, a successful CEO, and an award-winning landscape photographer whose work is featured internationally. He is also the author of *Inquire Within: A Guide to Living in Spirit.*

He resides in Washington State with his wife Lisa.

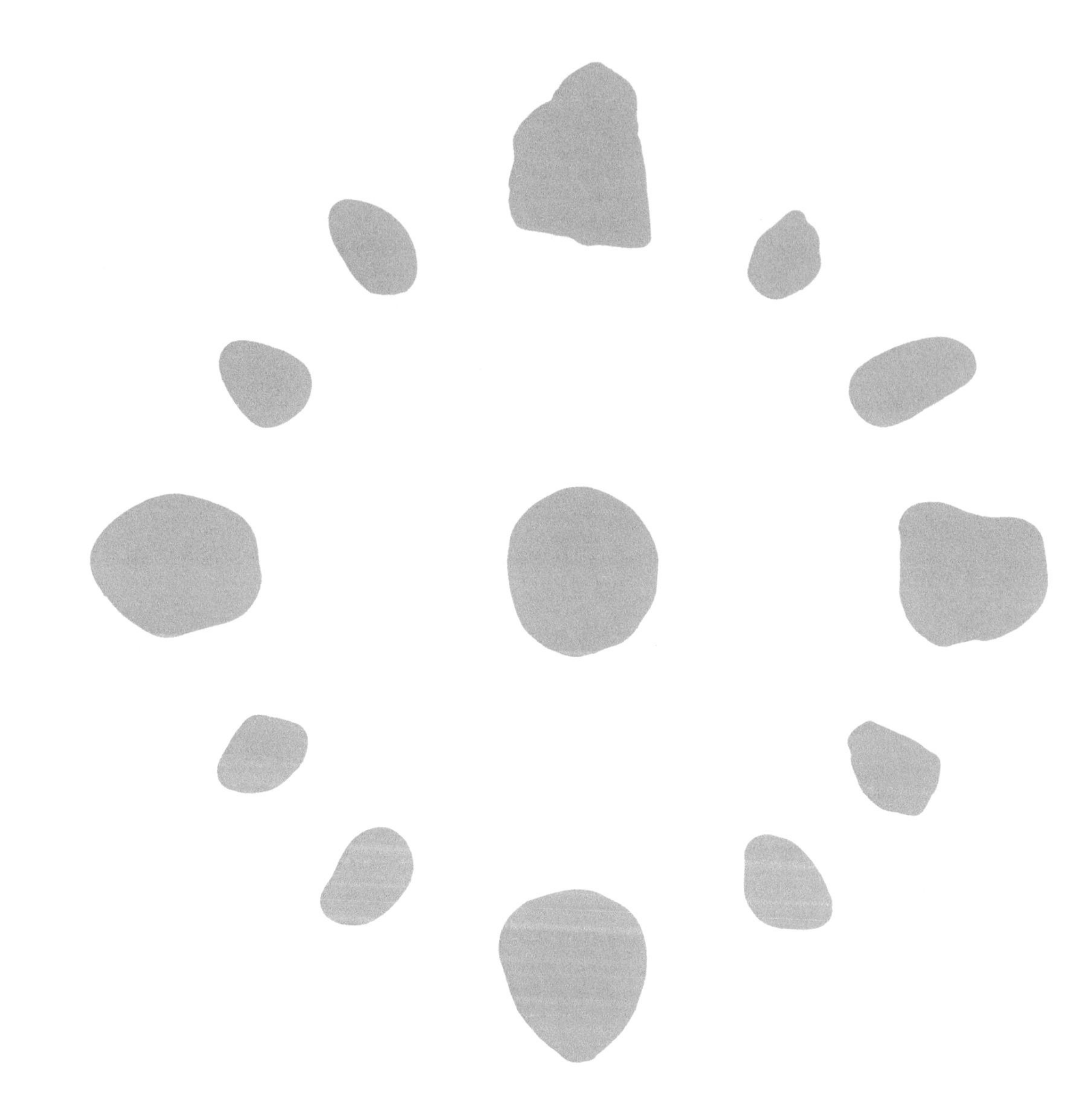